TATTERCOATS

Tattercoats

An old English Tale

Told by Flora Annie Steel

PICTURES BY DIANE GOODE

Bradbury Press   Scarsdale, New York

The text of this book is set in 16 pt. Goudy Old Style. The artist painted the pictures in water colors, using brushes on parchment. The illustrations are reproduced in full color.

David

all my love, always, Diane

N A GREAT PALACE BY THE SEA THERE ONCE DWELT A VERY RICH OLD LORD WHO HAD NEITHER WIFE NOR CHILDREN LIVING, ONLY ONE LITTLE GRANDDAUGHTER WHOSE FACE HE HAD NEVER SEEN IN ALL HER LIFE. HE hated her bitterly, because at her birth his favorite daughter died; and when the old nurse brought him the baby he swore that it might live or die as it liked, but he would never look on its face as long as it lived.

So he turned his back and sat by his window, looking out over the sea and weeping great tears for his lost daughter, till his white hair and beard grew down over his shoulders and twined round his chair and crept into the chinks of the floor, and his tears, dropping onto the window-ledge, wore a channel through the stone and ran away in a little river to the great sea.

Meanwhile, his granddaughter grew up with no one to care for her or clothe her; only the old nurse, when no one was by, would sometimes give her a dish of scraps from the kitchen or a torn petticoat from the ragbag; while the other servants of the palace would drive her from the house with blows and mocking words, calling her "Tatter-coats," and pointing to her bare feet and laughing, till she ran away crying, to hide among the bushes.

Tattercoats grew up with little to eat or to wear, spending her days out of doors, her only companion a crippled gooseherd, who fed his flock of geese on the common. This gooseherd was a queer, merry, little chap. When Tattercoats was hungry or cold or tired, he would play to her so gaily on his little pipe, that she forgot all her troubles and would fall to dancing with his flock of noisy geese for partners.

One day people told each other that the King was travelling through the land, and was to give a great ball to all the lords and ladies of the country in the town near by. The Prince, the King's only son, was to choose a wife from amongst the maidens in the company.

In due time, one of the royal invitations to the ball was brought to the palace by the sea. The servants carried it up to the old lord, who still sat by his window, wrapped in his long white hair and weeping into the little river that was fed by his tears.

When the old lord heard the King's command, he dried his eyes and bade his servants bring shears to cut him loose, for his hair had bound him a fast prisoner, and he could not move. Then he sent them for rich clothes and jewels, which he put on; and he ordered them to saddle the white horse with gold and silk, that he might ride to meet the King. But he quite forgot he had a granddaughter to take to the ball.

Tattercoats sat by the kitchen-door weeping, because she could not go to see the grand doings. And when the old nurse heard her crying, she went to the lord of the palace and begged him to take his granddaughter with him to the King's ball.

But he only frowned and told her to be silent; while the servants laughed and said, "Tattercoats is happy in her rags, playing with the gooseherd! Let her be—it is all she is fit for."

A second time, the old nurse begged him to let the girl go with him, but she was answered only by black looks and fierce words, till she was driven from the room.

Weeping over her ill-success, the old nurse went to look for Tat-tercoats; but the girl had been turned from the door by the cook, and had run away to tell her friend the gooseherd how unhappy she was because she could not go to the King's ball.

Now when the gooseherd had listened to her story, he bade her cheer up, and proposed that they should go together into the town to see the King and all the fine things. When she looked sorrowfully down at her rags and bare feet he played a note or two upon his pipe, so gay and merry, that she forgot all about her tears and her troubles. Before she well knew, the gooseherd had taken her by the hand, and she and he, with the geese before them, were dancing down the road towards the town.

Before they had gone very far, a handsome young man, splendidly dressed, rode up and asked the way to the castle where the King was staying. When he found that they too were going thither, he got off his horse and walked beside them along the road.

"You seem merry folk," he said, "and will be good company."

"Good company, indeed," said the gooseherd, and played a new tune that was not a dance.

It was a curious tune, and it made the strange young man stare and stare and stare at Tattercoats till he couldn't see her rags. Till he couldn't, to tell the truth, see anything but her beautiful face.

Then he said, "You are the most beautiful maiden in the world. Will you marry me?"

The gooseherd smiled to himself and played sweeter than ever.

But Tattercoats laughed. "Not I," said she, "you would be finely put to shame, and so would I be, if you took a goosegirl for your wife! Go and ask one of the great ladies you will see tonight at the King's ball and do not flout poor Tattercoats."

But the more she refused him the sweeter the pipe played, and the deeper the young man fell in love—till at last he begged her to come that night at twelve to the King's ball, just as she was, with the gooseherd and his geese, in her torn petticoat and bare feet, and see if he wouldn't dance with her before the King and the lords and ladies, and present her to them all as his dear and honored bride.

At first Tattercoats said she would not; but the gooseherd said, "Take fortune when it comes, little one."

When night came, the hall in the castle was full of light and music, and the lords and ladies were dancing before the King.

Just as the clock struck twelve, Tattercoats and the gooseherd, followed by his flock of noisy geese, entered at the great doors and walked straight up the ballroom, while on either side the ladies whispered, the lords laughed, and the King stared in amazement.

As they came in front of the throne, Tattercoats' lover rose from beside the King and came to meet her. Taking her by the hand, he kissed her thrice before them all, and turned to the King.

"Father!" he said—for it was the Prince himself—"I have made my choice, and here is my bride, the loveliest girl in all the land, and the sweetest as well!"

Before he had finished speaking, the gooseherd had put his pipe to his lips and played a few notes that sounded like a bird singing far off in the woods. And as he played, Tattercoats' rags were changed to shining robes sewn with glittering jewels, a golden crown lay upon her golden hair, and the flock of geese behind her became a crowd of pages, bearing her long train.

As the King rose to greet her as his daughter, the trumpets sounded loudly in honor of the new Princess and the people outside in the street said to each other:

"Ah! Now the Prince has chosen for his wife the loveliest girl in all the land!"

But the gooseherd was never seen again, and no one knew what became of him; while the old lord went home once more to his palace by the sea, for he could not stay at Court when he had sworn never to look on his granddaughter's face.

And there he still sits by his window, weeping more bitterly than ever. His white hair has bound him to the stones, and the river of his tears runs away to the great sea.